Dedicated to:

My husband Don and our four children:
Ian, Logan, Jason, and Megan.
They inspire my journey every day.

Dandy Lion

© 2014, Amy Klene

Author: Amy Klene
Illustrator: Amy Klene
Producer: Paul Pointer
ISBN: 978-1-312-28324-4

Four Fonts Used:

MOMS TYPEWRITER
Commercial Desktop Use
©1997 Christoph Mueller License v1.00
http://www.cuci.nl/~nonsuch/free.htm

AMATIC
Commercial Desktop Use
©2011 by Vernon Adams
(vern@newtypography.co.uk)
SIL Open Font License, Version 1.1.

LOBSTER
Commercial Desktop Use
Designed by: Impallari Type
SIL Open Font License v1.10

Caviar Dreams
Commercial & personal use.
©2009 by Lauren Thompson,
Nymphont License v1.00
http://nymphont.blogspot.com

Resource: FontSquirrel.com

Dandy Lion

Dandy Lion, Dandy Lion
turn around....

 1

I am so happy that
I've been...

2

FOUND

Dandy Lion, Dandy Lion
would you like to have...

 4

FUN

I found a big hill,
where we can...

 6

RUN

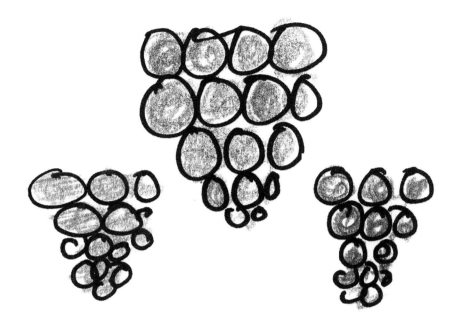

Dandy Lion, Dandy Lion
we had better eat some...

8

LUNCH

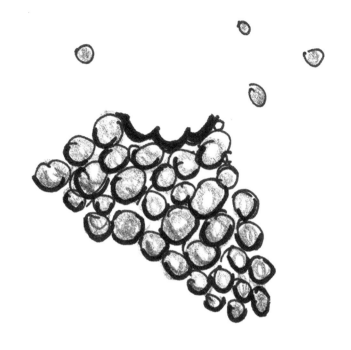

I have wild berries
that we can...

10

MUNCH

Dandy Lion, Dandy Lion
we had better take a...

12

NAP

Lay your head here
right in my soft green..

 14

LAP

15

Dandy Lion, Dandy Lion
your petals are
turning...

16

GREY

It's time for me to go
and start a new...

DAY

19

Dandy Lion, Dandy Lion
where will you...

20

GO

I will blow in the wind
but in your heart I will...

22

GROW

Dandy Lion, Dandy Lion
I will...

24

MISS

YOU

SO

25

I will be with
you always, so...

MAKE A WISH

AND...

28

BLOW

29 ♥

About the Author:

Amy Klene is a Colorado native and lives in the same town she grew up in. She went to the University of Northern Colorado and received a BA in English and Visual Art. She works full time as the Training Director for a technology company in Colorado and is a computer nerd. She loves writing, designing, laughing, and drinking coffee – not necessarily in that order. Her husband Don is the elementary school principal at the school she went to as a child. Her favorite thing to be is mom to her 3 children; Ian, Logan, and Megan. Her son Jason died as a baby and this book is largely a tribute to Jason and how those we love stay with us in our hearts always.